# HIP-HOP

50 Cent

Ashanti

Beyoncé

Mary J. Blige

Chris Brown

Mariah Carey

Sean "Diddy" Combs

Dr. Dre

Missy Elliott

Eminem

Hip-Hop: A Short History

Jay-Z

Alicia Keys

LL Cool J

Ludacris

Nelly

Notorious B.I.G.

Queen Latifah

Reverend Run (Run-D.M.C.)

Will Smith

Snoop Dogg

Tupac

Usher

Kanye West

Pharrell Williams

# Jay-Z

Geoffrey Barnes

Mason Crest Publishers

# Jay-Z

FRONTIS  From humble beginnings, Jay-Z helped to build a hip-hop music and fashion empire that has made him famous and wealthy.

PRODUCED BY 21ST CENTURY PUBLISHING AND COMMUNICATIONS, INC.

MASON CREST PUBLISHERS INC.
370 Reed Road
Broomall, Pennsylvania 19008
(866)MCP-BOOK (toll free)
www.masoncrest.com

Printed in the U.S.A.

First Printing

9 8 7 6 5 4 3 2 1

Library of Congress Cataloging-in-Publication Data

Barnes, Geoffrey, 1980–
  Jay-Z / Geoffrey Barnes.
    p. cm. — (Hip-hop)
  Includes bibliographical references and index.
  Hardback edition: ISBN-13: 978-1-4222-0119-0
  Hardback edition: ISBN-10: 1-4222-0119-8
  Paperback edition: ISBN-13: 978-1-4222-0269-2
  1. Jay-Z, 1970–   —Juvenile literature. 2. Rap musicians—United States—
Biography—Juvenile literature. I. Title. II. Series.
ML3930.J38B36 2007
782.421649092—dc22
[B]                                                      2006017327

*Publisher's notes:*
- All quotations in this book come from original sources, and contain the spelling and grammatical inconsistencies of the original text.

- The Web sites mentioned in this book were active at the time of publication. The publisher is not responsible for Web sites that have changed their addresses or discontinued operation since the date of publication. The publisher will review and update the Web site addresses each time the book is reprinted.

# Contents

Hip-Hop Timeline                                          6

**1** A Farewell Party                                    9

**2** Early Days in Marcy                                15

**3** Roc-A-Fella Records                                23

**4** Stardom                                            29

**5** Trouble in Paradise                                37

**6** Retiring from Rap                                  47

Chronology                                               56

Accomplishments & Awards                                 58

Further Reading & Internet Resources                     60

Glossary                                                 61

Index                                                    62

Picture Credits                                          64

About the Author                                         64

# Hip-Hop Timeline

**1974** Hip-hop pioneer Afrika Bambaataa organizes the Universal Zulu Nation.

**1988** *Yo! MTV Raps* premieres on MTV.

**1970s** Hip-hop as a cultural movement begins in the Bronx, New York City.

**1985** *Krush Groove*, a hip-hop film about Def Jam Recordings, is released featuring Run-D.M.C., Kurtis Blow, LL Cool J, and the Beastie Boys.

**1970s** DJ Kool Herc pioneers the use of breaks, isolations, and repeats using two turntables.

**1979** The Sugarhill Gang's song "Rapper's Delight" is the first hip-hop single to go gold.

**1986** Run-D.M.C. are the first rappers to appear on the cover of *Rolling Stone* magazine.

## 1970          1980          1988

**1976** Grandmaster Flash & the Furious Five pioneer hip-hop MCing and freestyle battles.

**1986** Beastie Boys' album *Licensed to Ill* is released and becomes the best-selling rap album of the 1980s.

**1970s** Break dancing emerges at parties and in public places in New York City.

**1982** Afrika Bambaataa embarks on the first European hip-hop tour.

**1988** Hip-hop music annual record sales reaches $100 million.

**1970s** Graffiti artist Vic pioneers tagging on subway trains in New York City.

**1984** *Graffiti Rock*, the first hip-hop television program, premieres.

**1993** Rapper Snoop Dogg's album *Doggystyle* is the first debut album to hit the music charts at number one.

**2006** Queen Latifah becomes the first hip-hop artist to receive a star on the Hollywood Walk of Fame.

**1989** DJ Jazzy Jeff & The Fresh Prince become the first hip-hop artists to win a Grammy Award.

**2003** Rapper Eminem becomes the first hip-hop artist to win an Academy Award.

**2005** Hip-hop artist Kanye West appears on the cover of *Time* magazine.

**1989** Rap is added as a new category to the *Billboard* charts.

**1997** East Coast rapper Notorious B.I.G. (aka Biggie Smalls) is murdered.

**2004** First National Hip-Hop Political Convention is held in Newark, New Jersey.

## 1989　　　　　　2000　　　　　　2006

**1990s** Hip-hop emerges in Europe.

**1996** West Coast rapper Tupac Shakur is shot and killed.

**2005** Rapper Will Smith opens the Philadelphia Live 8 concert as part of 10 simultaneous concerts held worldwide to bring attention to the extreme poverty in Africa.

**1989** First gangsta rap album, *Straight Outta Compton*, is released by N.W.A.

**2001** The hip-hop political action group, Hip-Hop Summit Action Network, is founded by Russell Simmons.

**1992** Dr. Dre's album *The Chronic* is released; it redefines West Coast rap.

**2006** The Smithsonian Institute National Museum of American History announces the creation of a new hip-hop exhibition scheduled to open in three to five years.

Rapper Jay-Z attends the New York premiere of the film *Fade to Black* in November 2004. The documentary focuses on events around the release of his critically acclaimed *Black Album* (2003), which was supposed to be the rapper's final album.

# 1

# A Farewell Party

New York's Madison Square Garden is one of the most coveted stages in the world. On November 25, 2003, a young man from Brooklyn, who as a child could not have afforded to go to a basketball game there, made his first appearance at the Garden in a "farewell concert" before more than 20,000 screaming fans.

Having just released what he claimed was his final album as a recording artist, rapper Shawn Carter, known popularly as Jay-Z, threw a concert called Fade to Black. Dubbed his "retirement party," the concert was intended to cap off his short but wildly successful career as a performer. "Jay's status appears to be at an all-time high," he raps on *The Black Album*. "[It is the] perfect time to say good-bye."

For years management at Madison Square Garden had not allowed hip-hop on its stage. In part the arena's handlers feared the violent reputation of hip-hop crowds, but many have speculated they were also concerned that hip-hop shows could not earn enough to justify using such a huge space. Rock and pop acts and major sporting events like New York Knicks games were much more profitable for the arena. It made no sense to block out time for a show that would bring in less money. However, when tickets went on sale for Jay-Z's final concert—the first rap concert in nearly 15 years to grace the stage—these concerns proved unfounded. The world-famous arena sold out in less than five minutes, and the show went off without incident.

Kevin Lyles, president of Warner Music Group, admits in the film *Fade to Black*, "I don't know another artist who could sell out the Garden in a day." The event was memorable. And the wide variety of famous faces in attendance was evidence of Jay's influence on popular culture. ?uestlove, the drummer from the hip-hop band The Roots, played with Jay at the show. He says in the *Fade to Black* documentary, "I think what made it historical was that people from all walks of life were there to rock with him." "His album [was] two weeks old," marvels his long-time friend and collaborator DJ Clark Kent in the film. "It was like everybody there knew the words to every song."

## The Stuff of Dreams

Jay-Z had grown up in Brooklyn, looking across the East River at Manhattan, dreaming of being one of New York City's elite. Like nothing he had done before, the concert at the Garden confirmed that he had achieved this goal. All his dreams had come true. As Damon Dash, his long-time friend and business partner, recalls, "I remember him telling me what he was gonna do [play Madison Square Garden] ten years prior to that."

The star-studded event was brimming with famous entertainers, yet, as CNN's pop correspondent Toure says in *Fade to Black*, "He's still the main attraction. Nobody can blot out the sun that is Jay-Z." That night Jay-Z shared his stage with the likes of Mary J. Blige, Beyoncé Knowles, Missy Elliott, and Foxy Brown. He changed his outfit five times and ran a song list not just from his latest album, but one that spanned his entire career. There was a **pyrotechnics** show, and the famous fight announcer Michael Buffer introduced him. Q-Tip, a member of the rap group A Tribe Called Quest, recalls in the film, "You knew before it started that this was gonna be something special."

**Jay-Z performs with his girlfriend, R&B superstar Beyoncé, on the stage at Madison Square Garden during the "Fade to Black" concert on November 25, 2003. The star-studded concert was meant to mark Jay-Z's retirement as a hip-hop performer.**

## Rise to the Top

In eight years Jay-Z had released nine full-length albums, worked on four collaborative albums, and helped to create an empire based in entertainment and fashion. He was estimated to be worth more than $300 million, a distinction that gained him a spot on *Forbes* magazine's "Forty under Forty" list. He had been dating one of the most successful

Many people consider Jay-Z, shown here at a 2003 concert, to be the best rapper alive. In fact, a 2006 article published by MTV named him the greatest rapper of all time, ranking him ahead of such stars as Tupac and the Notorious B.I.G.

R&B singers ever, Beyoncé Knowles, for close to four years. As he puts it in his song "PSA": "[I've] got the hottest chick in the game wearin' my chain." Jay-Z had sold more than 30 million records, started a scholarship fund, bought a piece of an NBA team, scouted and developed platinum-selling recording artists, and started a film company. Known as "Hov," "Jigga," and "J-Hova," he also laid claim to the title "Best Rapper Alive" and fiercely defended it from many challengers.

Over the years, the 33-year-old rapper had faced his share of difficulties and disappointments. He had started out poor, selling drugs to make a living. He had faced imprisonment for assault, been sued and picketed against, and had his life threatened repeatedly. He had buried a friend, a nephew, and his father, all in view of the public.

Despite these difficulties, in less than a decade Jay had risen from a virtual unknown to an international superstar, philanthropist, and business mogul. "From Marcy to Madison Square," he raps in "Encore," a single from *The Black Album*, "it's just a matter of years." He and his business partners Damon Dash and Kareem Burke had realized the American dream. It was not an easy road, and for many of his fans, his resilience and confidence are what make him a hip-hop icon. His protégé, Memphis Bleek, offers an explanation for Jay's folk hero status in the film documenting the night: "I've known Jay all my life. We come from Marcy Projects. We lived off of food stamps. . . . It's like going from the bottom to the Promised Land."

Shawn Carter, who would later gain fame under the stage name Jay-Z, had a difficult childhood. He grew up in a decaying housing project in Brooklyn. The Carter family was poor, and Shawn's home life was unstable.

# 2

# Early Days in Marcy

**J**ay-Z was born Shawn Corey Carter on December 4, 1970, in Brooklyn, New York. The youngest of four children, he grew up in the Bedford-Stuyvesant section of Brooklyn. Shawn's family lived in Marcy Houses, a public housing project for low-income families. Marcy was a tough neighborhood, and it sharpened his street smarts early on.

From a young age, Shawn was a bit of a show-off, and his neighbors took to calling him "Jazzy." "I had the same demeanor as I do now: I was a cool kid, a jazzy little dude," he remarked as an adult. In 2006 he recalled the first time he tasted fame: "It was really high, but I put my foot through the top bar [of a 10-speed bicycle], so I'm ridin' the bike sideways and the whole block is like, 'Oh God;' they couldn't believe [I] was riding this bike like that. That was my first feelin' of bein' famous." Later the nickname "Jazzy" was shortened to Jay-Z.

Shawn's mother, Gloria, was an investment company clerk. She became the sole provider for her family when Shawn's father, Adnis Reeves, left. Shawn was 11 years old when his father moved out, and he was never the same. He admits freely that his father leaving home hurt him deeply. "Kids look up to they pop like Superman," he later said. "Superman just left [home]? . . . That's traumatic."

## Dealing Drugs

Life in the Marcy projects was hard, and few people had the money or education to improve their lives. To escape from their everyday problems, many people used drugs like marijuana, heroin, and cocaine. As a result, selling drugs was a potentially lucrative business for young urban men.

While Shawn was growing up, a new drug was becoming popular among poor drug users in American cities: crack cocaine. The money that could be made from selling crack was hard for dealers like Shawn to resist. Crack is made by combining cocaine with baking soda, hydrogen hydroxide, and other ingredients. This creates a crystallike substance that can then be chipped into small doses, which can be smoked for a short but powerful high. Crack is cheaper than regular powder cocaine, so it became known as a "poor man's drug." However, crack proved to be severely addictive, and it ruined the lives of many people who could not break their dependence.

Crack, and the addicts it produced, infested American ghettos in the mid-1980s. The Marcy housing project was no exception. Motivated by the sight of other young men providing themselves with lives of relative luxury, Shawn and many poor kids like him turned to dealing drugs for cash. "There was no other way," he later said.

Shawn was always aware that selling drugs was not a long-term solution to poverty. He knew from watching others that sooner or later he would either wind up in jail or become a victim of the violence that surrounds the drug trade. "I've seen this story play out a million times," he later said to *Teen People*. He needed to find another way.

## Short- and Long-term Plans

Shawn had always been interested in music, and as a young man he was enthralled by hip-hop. In the streets where he spent most of his time as a teen, he didn't carry a notebook to write down the rhymes he invented. Instead he memorized everything, eventually developing the ability to compose and store whole songs without ever writing them down. Singer Beyoncé Knowles told *Vanity Fair* in 2005 that Jay was still able to craft rhymes the way he had in his hustling days:

> **"He just sits there and his mouth starts moving silently, and all of a sudden he does this rap . . . without writing anything down."**

Convinced that he was as good or better than most of the new talent coming onto the rap scene in the late 1980s, Jay-Z began to look toward a career in music as his way out of Marcy. He began to build a

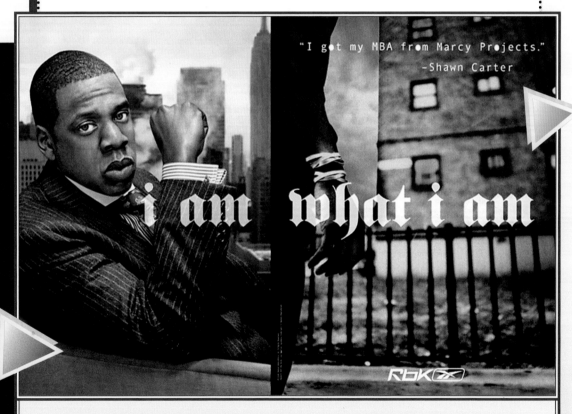

"I got my MBA from Marcy Projects."
-Shawn Carter

i am what i am

RBK

**"I got my MBA from Marcy Projects," says Shawn Carter in this sneaker advertisement. The rapper was apparently referring to the business skills he learned while selling drugs in the projects. Although being a dealer was lucrative, Shawn found that it could also be dangerous.**

friendship with a rapper named Jaz-O, whom he had met through his dealings with another rapper, Big Daddy Kane. Jaz-O helped teach him how to navigate the record industry. He even invited Jay-Z to contribute to a record he made called "Hawaiian Sophie," which became a minor hit.

Jay appeared on a few more records with members from Original Flavor, an easily forgotten trio of rappers from New York. He outshone them at every turn and continued to build a following with his release of the song "Show and Prove," which featured Big Daddy Kane and several other rappers. None of the early acts hit it big, but through them Jay was meeting plenty of people in the music business. One such contact was DJ Clark Kent, a producer and DJ from the New York area. Kent was impressed with Jay from the moment they met. "When [Jay] was 15 he wanted to be the best rapper," he remembers. "It's funny how effortlessly it came to him."

But rapping wasn't as profitable as hustling drugs. So even when Kent offered to pay for and produce Jay's music, it was difficult for Jay to accept a career that paid less. Kent did, however, introduce Jay to a young promoter from Harlem who would help him focus and achieve stardom: Damon Dash.

## A New Hustle

Damon Dash was a small-time music manager and party promoter from Harlem, a middle-class black enclave on Manhattan Island. Though he also came from a broken home, Dash had a relatively privileged upbringing, attending private prep schools on need-based and academic scholarships. He developed a track record for being a shrewd business-man in East Harlem when he began hosting parties in the early 1990s to fund his music management business.

Early on Dash had grand ambitions of starting a string of busi-nesses anchored in music, fashion, and marketing. He was convinced that hip-hop culture could be a commercial success outside of the music industry. Dash used parties and other engagements to promote his artists; he then used the artists to promote forthcoming events. Later Dash, Jay, and their business partners would use this **cross-marketing** practice to help launch the Rocawear clothing line. It allowed them to make money off of every aspect of the culture, from what hip-hop listeners watched to what they wore to even what they drank. Dash justified his strategy to *Fortune Small Business* in 2004:

Shawn had an unusual skill at composing rhymes in his head without writing them down. He soon developed this ability, and was able to memorize entire songs, a feat that amazed people involved in the music industry who heard him rapping.

> **"We [the hip hop community] shouldn't let other people make money off of us, and we shouldn't give free advertising with our lifestyle."**

In other words, entertainers should be compensated by the companies and brands that they make popular.

In order to start his career in marketing, Dash tried his hand at rapping. "If I could rap to sell my [products], I would. We'd be way

**In 1995 Damon "Dame" Dash offered to manage Jay-Z's music career. Dash was a shrewd businessman and entrepreneur who had a plan to develop a hip-hop music and fashion empire. He considered Shawn a talented performer who could help him promote various products and interests.**

ahead, and I wouldn't have to work as hard," he said. But he wasn't much of a recording artist and needed to find better talent to help him realize his dream. He was impressed by Jay's abilities as a rapper and in 1995 signed him to a management deal.

Jay-Z was still selling drugs and was therefore far from a "starving artist" when Dash signed him. The drug business was no easy job, though, and Jay was beginning to tire of the constant worry that comes with engaging in such a dangerous and illegal enterprise.

**❝By the age of 22 I knew I had to get out [of the drug business] because the only future is jail or die,❞**

he remembered. But he had grown accustomed to the lifestyle that drug money provided, and it wasn't until he was signed to a label that he was willing to give up selling.

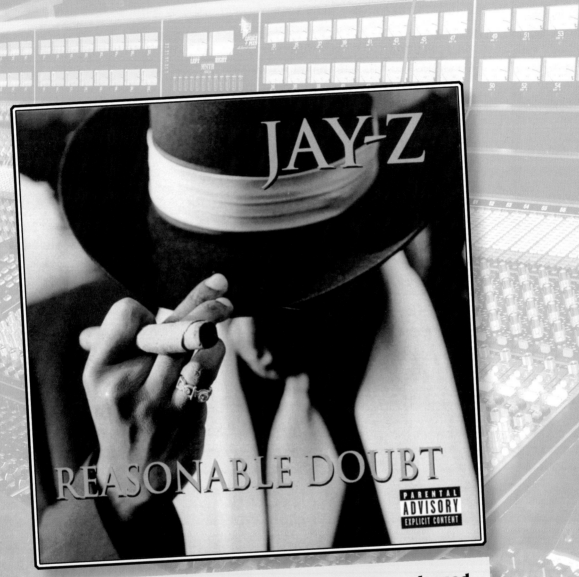

Jay-Z's first album, *Reasonable Doubt*, was released in 1996 to critical acclaim but relatively slow sales. Today, most music critics consider *Reasonable Doubt* a groundbreaking album that helped influence the direction of rap music during the 1990s.

# 3

# Roc-A-Fella Records

Jay's management deal with Dash ultimately proved to be a turning point in his life. Dash had such high expectations for his newfound client that he paid to produce Jay's first album, *Reasonable Doubt.* The expense was small by industry standards, but would have been staggering to an independent artist without Dash's resources.

Their friend Kareem "Biggs" Burke also invested in the project, and this helped Jay-Z and Dash to enlist talented performers to contribute to the album. Jay's friend DJ Clark Kent provided beats and produced several songs, and a well-known rapper from Brooklyn, Notorious B.I.G., joined Jay-Z on the track "Brooklyn's Finest." B.I.G. was an influential rapper—he is considered by many hip-hop fans to be among the best ever—and he and Jay-Z became friends.

Once the album was done, Dash began offering Jay-Z's music to New York record companies. Everyone turned him down. After a frustrating year, Jay, Dash, and Burke decided to form their own company, Roc-A-Fella

Records, and distribute the album themselves. While many now consider their decision to start a record company a shrewd attempt to cut out the middleman, Jay admits that it was not his business partners' first choice. "I wish we could take credit for thinkin' of that on our own," he recalls, "but it was more . . . [that] after a year of shoppin' I was like, 'Man, let's put it out ourself.'"

## Do-It-Yourself Wealth

Established in early 1996, Roc-A-Fella Records was one of a growing number of independent hip-hop record labels opting to go it on their own. Other **boutique** labels that became dominant forces in the entertainment world include Bad Boy Records, No Limit Records, and G Unit Records.

*Reasonable Doubt* was not a huge commercial success, but it did attract attention. Jay's first single, "Ain't No Nigga," a collaboration with Foxy Brown, introduced audiences to a playful and witty playboy. His follow-up singles "Dead Presidents" and "Can't Knock the Hustle" showed them an inexhaustible hustler. And songs such as "22 Twos" introduced them to a polished technician and wordsmith.

Thanks to an arrangement with Priority Records to distribute the album to record stores, *Reasonable Doubt* eventually went **gold**. This success helped convince Dash, Jay, and Biggs that instead of giving Jay's music away to a major label, they could use him to become a major label themselves. They began looking for an arrangement with other record companies that would help them to grow.

Eventually, they signed a deal with Def Jam Recordings, famed in the hip-hop world as the first rap label to achieve significant success. Over the years Def Jam had promoted some of the most important rap acts in the world, including Run-D.M.C., LL Cool J, and A Tribe Called Quest. In the **joint venture** deal they offered to Roc-A-Fella, everything, including ownership of the **masters** to Jay-Z's music, was evenly split between the two companies. The deal made Jay-Z a professional rapper who could leave the drug business behind forever.

## Regional Conflict

Leaving drugs behind, however, did not mean leaving danger entirely behind. For years rappers from different geographic regions had developed unique styles. During the mid-1990s, though, a well-publicized rivalry between two record labels on opposite coasts took

**Damon Dash, Jay-Z, and Biggs Burke are shown together at the Rocawear 2002 Fall Fashion Show in New York City. The three men established the hip-hop music label Roc-A-Fella Records in 1995 to distribute Jay-Z's first album.**

the regional competition to a new level. By 1996 tensions between rappers from the West Coast and rappers from the East Coast had reached an all-time high.

Tupac Shakur and Jay-Z's friend Notorious B.I.G. were the centerpieces of this rivalry, trading insults through their music. Tupac was signed to a label called Death Row Records, which boasted a roster that included such stars as Snoop Dogg and Dr. Dre. In the early 1990s,

Los Angeles–based Death Row had become a powerhouse, defining the West Coast sound and selling millions of albums. On the East Coast, the label most comparable was Bad Boy, for which Notorious B.I.G. was the **marquee** talent. Run by Sean "Puffy" Combs, Bad Boy signified a revival for New York rap music.

As the two labels battled for supremacy on the radio, some of the violence they depicted in their music became a reality. After Tupac was shot in the lobby of a recording studio in New York in 1994, he suggested that B.I.G. and Bad Boy had been responsible. Though Notorious B.I.G. denied any involvement, his song "Who Shot Ya?" didn't help soothe matters.

**Jay-Z did not want to be drawn into the rivalry between Tupac (left) and Notorious B.I.G. Jay-Z was friendly with B.I.G., who had contributed vocals to *Reasonable Doubt*, and saddened when the rapper was murdered in March 1997.**

In 1995 Tupac released "Hit 'Em Up," an insulting song aimed not only at Notorious B.I.G. and Bad Boy, but almost every New York rapper who had even casually aligned themselves with B.I.G., including Jay-Z. In his lyrics Tupac claimed that he had slept with B.I.G.'s wife, Faith Evans, and even ridiculed Mobb Deep member Tragedy, who suffered from sickle cell anemia, for his poor health.

Within two years both Tupac and Notorious B.I.G. had died violent deaths, which are to this day unsolved. Many people believe their deaths were directly linked to the music they made. And many in the industry wanted rap music to return to its more simple times, when conflicts were settled on the microphone instead of with guns.

Jay had lost a friend when the Notorious B.I.G. was gunned down in March 1997. He also knew that he did not want to contribute to the feud, because as a relatively new artist he had nothing to gain by alienating listeners or endangering his own life. Instead, he concentrated on recording his second full-length album, hoping for continued success.

Jay-Z pauses on stage during a 1997 concert. That year, he released his second album, *In My Lifetime, Vol. 1*. Although some fans complained that the record sounded more commercial than *Reasonable Doubt*, *In My Lifetime* sold more than a million copies.

# 4

# Stardom

By 1997 Jay was poised for success. His debut was still circulating to critical acclaim, and his follow-up album was well underway. The murder of the Notorious B.I.G. had left the hip-hop community searching for someone to take his place. Even though Jay was sad about his friend's death, he hoped that someone would be him.

Jay's second album, *In My Lifetime, Vol. 1*, was a departure from *Reasonable Doubt*. The first album had been a dark and gritty series of tales full of gangster motifs and thoughtful meditations on street life. With singles such as "The City is Mine," featuring a **sample** from pop star Glenn Frey, *Vol. 1* was clearly a drive for a wider pop audience.

Many of Jay's initial fans felt slighted by the obvious attempt to reach another market. They accused him of becoming a "sellout." Jay and his new associates at Def Jam were all too aware that criticism like this would come, and in producing the album they had tried to strike a balance between hardcore rap and pop music. One executive at Def Jam summed up their strategy to *Billboard* this way: "The overall plan is to increase his visibility and make him that crossover artist without sacrificing his full street credibility."

Jay maintained that critics of the album did not understand what he was trying to do. Instead of an effort to "cross over," Jay claimed that the new sound was part of an effort to reveal a new maturity in his character. Speaking of the shift from his debut to his second effort, he told *Billboard*:

> **"I want people to compare the two albums to a relationship with a girl . . . When you meet her, it's physical. . . . The first album dealt with things on the outside . . . things you could see."**

On the second album, he said:

> **"I'm gonna take 'em a little deeper. Now we can explore and get to the heart of Jay-Z."**

However, critics were quick to point out that most of *In My Lifetime* lacked depth, and that Jay had opted instead to exhibit more "surface" than before. Years later even Jay himself would agree that *Vol. 1* was too pop-oriented. When asked in 2006 in an online chat which of all his albums he would change, he admitted:

> **"I would change Volume 1. It was so close to being a classic with songs like Streets is Watchin, Where I'm From, You Must Love Me, Lucky Me, etc. . . . I think I ruined it with two or three [songs]."**

Often Jay's rhymes were filled with violent, **materialistic**, and **misogynistic** references, which drew the ire of those who wanted to see rap go in a new direction after the murders of Tupac and B.I.G. There are moments, however, where he drops the outward show and does some soul-searching, as promised.

On one song, "Lucky Me," Jay discusses the perils of fame and how uncomfortable it can be. He wanted his listeners to be able to recognize that he still had problems even though he seemed so successful. In his lyrics he complains:

Wearing a bulletproof vest, Jay-Z performs at a concert in Massachusetts, 1997. In his song "Lucky Me," the rapper discusses the price of fame, including his fear that he might be gunned down just as Tupac and Notorious B.I.G. had been.

> " Every day I'm dealing with stress.
> Got up out the streets, you'd think a [person] could rest.
> Can't even enjoy myself at a party unless I'm on the dance floor, [wearing a] hot [bulletproof] vest. "

Jay still feared for his life, even though he was an entertainer instead of a drug dealer.

## Making Amends

With respect to the still-raw relations beween East and West Coast rappers, Jay made it a point to reach out to a California artist of some clout—Too $hort. Their collaboration on *In My Lifetime* symbolized a larger trend among hip-hop artists, who realized that the rivalry had gone too far. In the last verse from their song "Real Niggaz," Jay did his part in mending East-West relations, rapping: "I want Biggie to rest in peace, as well as Pac." By acknowledging that both Tupac and Notorious B.I.G. were worthy of respect, Jay attempted to put the conflict to rest for good.

He also appeased some of his original fan base with offerings like "Rap Game/Crack Game," a song in which he compares his two careers. Jay draws parallels between the two in a dramatic show of lyrical and conceptual **dexterity**. From product development to marketing to controlling demand, he explains how similar being a drug dealer is to being a recording artist and executive. By comparing it to a legitimate career, he asks his audience to question whether the drug industry is an "easy way" to make money, given the possible penalty.

Despite the criticism, *In My Lifetime, Vol. 1* was a successful album, selling more than a million copies. As a result, Jay-Z's career was taking off. With his second album climbing the charts, Jay appeared to be on his way to becoming the new statesman of New York hip-hop. Roc-A-Fella Records was expanding, adding new talent, and Jay was teetering on the edge of superstardom. His next move would push him over the edge.

## Superstardom

In the spring of 1998, Jay-Z unveiled *Vol. 2: Hard Knock Life*. The first single, "Hard-Knock Life (Ghetto Anthem)," became his biggest hit yet, and the album was his first to debut in the number-one spot on *Billboard's* pop chart. With a loop sampled from the Broadway musical *Annie* serving as the chorus, combined with Jay's signature conversational flow, the song captured audiences everywhere and dominated the airwaves for the bulk of the summer.

Though the sample, from the *Annie* song "It's a Hard Knock Life," was "soft" by any standard and the song was certainly more pop-oriented than anything he had done to date, in his lyrics Jay was careful to align himself with his core audience. "I flow for chicks wishin' they ain't have to strip to pay tuition," he spoke in verse, before vowing, "Hustling's still inside of me." He was again defending his hardcore, ghetto-bred reputation, but in a more playful and confident way.

The follow-up singles took off as well, with innovative beats by the hottest producers of the day like Timbaland, Kid Capri, and Just Blaze. "Jigga What," "Money Ain't a Thing," and "Can I Get a . . ." stayed at the top of the US and UK charts for weeks at a time and propelled the album's sales to quadruple platinum. Jay kept up his tradition of having popular guest rappers on his records, trading verses with his long-time collaborator Foxy Brown and later with Atlanta producer and rapper Jermaine Dupri. He also hosted DMX and Ja Rule, continued a storyline first developed on *Reasonable Doubt* with his protégé Memphis Bleek, and introduced a new female addition to the Roc-A-Fella roster: Amil. He even included his mentor Jaz-O and a former collaborator from his Original Flavor days, Sauce Money.

## Dealing with Criticism

There were so many additional artists that some of his critics took issue with them. Of the 14 songs on *Hard Knock Life*, Jay-Z raps by himself on just two. Every other song features at least one other artist, leading many people to complain that he had been crowded out of his own album.

In addition to those complaints, Jay's increasing popularity was making him a key target for critics outside of the rap world, who took issue with his gangster-themed lyrics. They were concerned about the influence he might have over his young listeners. One review of *Hard Knock Life* by Focus on the Family, a Christian group that surveys popular culture, cautioned parents:

**"If teens embrace his views on sex, drugs and solving conflict, they're in for a hard knock life of their own. Avoid this garbage at all costs!"**

This was certainly not the first time gangsta rap had been targeted by people concerned about its effects on young and impressionable listeners, but Jay-Z found that as he became more popular, the scrutiny would increase.

Jay ignored his critics. *Hard Knock Life* eventually sold more than 5 million copies, making it his best-selling album ever. To promote *Hard Knock Life*, Jay began a grueling 52-city national tour. He was joined on tour by several other rap stars, including Redman, Method Man, DMX, and Ja Rule. At the time the Hard Knock Life Tour was the most successful all hip-hop tour ever, selling out in every city it passed through. Despite the concerns of a few people, who feared that violence would erupt, the concert series was largely peaceful. Jay even donated

**Memphis Bleek (left) poses with Jay-Z at the Rocawear 2002 Fall Fashion Show in New York. Like Jay-Z, Memphis grew up in Brooklyn's Marcy projects, and he contributed lyrics to several of Jay-Z's albums. Memphis has also released several solo albums.**

some of the tour's proceeds to a charity fund established to help survivors of the 1999 Columbine High School shootings in Colorado.

As 1998 closed it was clear that Jay-Z had gained great respect within the music industry. However, he still felt annoyed that rap music was often overlooked or ignored by the mainstream media. In 1999, when *Hard Knock Life* won a Grammy Award for Best Rap Album, Jay-Z accepted the award but chose not to attend the ceremony because the Best Rap Album segment would not be televised.

He explained in a letter to the Associated Press:

> **"I am boycotting the Grammy Awards because too many major rap artists continue to be overlooked."**

## Building an Empire

Jay also had his sights set on being more than a music icon. In 1999 Roc-A-Fella Records established Rocawear, an urban fashion line. As Damon Dash recalled, "We always wanted to go into clothing, it was just a matter of the opportunity presenting itself." Jay and partner "Biggs" Burke agreed that they couldn't have launched a new company at a better time—Jay was at his most popular and influential.

As the Roc-A-Fella Records family continued to grow, breakout artists like Beanie Sigel and Freeway appeared alongside Jay in videos and at tour dates draped head-to-toe in Rocawear clothing. Just as before, when they used parties to promote the music and music to promote the parties, Dash's cross-marketing approach worked wonders. The success of the clothing line increased the visibility of Roc-A-Fella Records artists, and helped make Jay-Z and his partners very wealthy in the process.

*Vol. 3: Life and Times of S. Carter*, Jay-Z's fourth album, was another huge success. The record debuted in the top spot on *Billboard*'s album chart, spawned the hit single "Big Pimpin'," and eventually sold several million copies.

# 5

## Trouble in Paradise

**B**y 1999, it seemed like Jay's songs were always on the radio. Roc-A-Fella was adding talent to its roster, and Rocawear clothing sales were growing. And that year Jay's fourth album, *Vol. 3: Life and Times of S. Carter*, debuted at number one and stayed there for weeks, further cementing his superstar status.

The first single off *Life and Times* was "Big Pimpin," a bouncy pop song that seemed to include everything Jay-Z had been criticized for in the past. The lyrics were misogynistic, the sound was commercial, and Jay-Z was joined by several guest rappers. None of that seemed to matter. "Big Pimpin'" became a big hit, and reached number one on MTV's Top 40 chart by the end of the year.

In his lyrics, Jay continued his balancing act between hardcore fans and commercial interests. He argued that he was not a sell-out to corporate interests but rather a representative for poor blacks everywhere. Speaking directly to audiences from impoverished neighborhoods like Marcy, he rapped:

> **"I ain't crossover, I brought the suburbs to the hood
> Made em relate to your struggle, told em bout
>     your hustle
> Went on MTV with do-rags, I made them love you."**

## Legal Matters

After the release of his fourth album, Jay was involved in a bar brawl in New York in which an executive from another rap label was stabbed in the stomach. The star-studded event, an industry party for rapper Q-Tip of A Tribe Called Quest, took place at the Kit Kat Club on Times Square. The victim was Lance "Un" Rivera, the CEO of Undeas Entertainment.

Accounts of the night remain muddled, but at some point, a scuffle broke out in the VIP section of the club. Un was stabbed repeatedly in the stomach and bludgeoned with a champagne bottle. He later filed a lawsuit claiming that Shawn "Jay-Z" Carter had been the attacker.

In addition to the civil lawsuit, which would force Jay to pay for damages if he were convicted, New York prosecutors decided to file criminal charges against him for assault. If Jay were convicted in the criminal case, he could face up to 15 years in prison. The prosecutors **subpoenaed** witnesses from the Kit Kat Club to prove their case against the rapper. Jay maintained his innocence, saying that he had no problem with Un or his associates. He cited a video taken at the club as evidence that he was nowhere near Un when the stabbing took place.

As the civil suit got underway in 2000, Un's story began to waver. He claimed that he could no longer be sure that Jay-Z was the person who stabbed him. The details of the evening were hazy. The criminal prosecutors working on the case were nervous about moving forward with Un's shaky testimony.

Jay spent a lot of money on lawyers, hoping to stay out of jail. For close to two years, while the investigation went on and the case was prepared, Jay tried to stay out of trouble. Reflecting on the incident he told *People*:

> **"I felt like I was untouchable, but [the incident at the Kit Kat Club] let me see that it could all go away in an instant."**

Although Un eventually withdrew his civil complaint, Jay was still facing a criminal trial. Just as it was about to begin, though, the prosecutors offered Jay a **plea agreement**. If Jay would plead guilty to a lesser charge, he would get no jail time but three years' probation. He accepted the offer, explaining that he did not feel comfortable taking the risk of being convicted just to prove his innocence.

"Where I grew up, I saw a lot of people get wronged. No matter how much you believe in the truth, that's always in the back of your mind."

Shawn Carter is arrested for his involvement in a nightclub dispute that ended with a record company executive being stabbed. Ultimately, police were not sure they had enough evidence to convict Jay-Z, and the rapper avoided trial by pleading guilty to a lesser charge.

## Roc La Familia

Despite the legal trouble, Jay had managed to release another album, which hit number one by year's end. It was the first time in 25 years an artist had had two number one albums in the same year. Entitled *The Dynasty: Roc La Familia*, the album served mostly as a platform to promote other talent on the Roc-A-Fella label such as Amil, Memphis Bleek, and Beanie Sigel. Industry critics tore it to pieces. Again many fans were disappointed by the scarcity of Jay's voice as he made way for his labelmates to establish themselves.

As always, though, there were a few high points. "Where Have You Been?," in which Jay and Beanie Sigel address their missing fathers, marked the first time Jay shared his pain over being abandoned in a song. "Do you even remember December's my birthday?" Jay asks in his verse. Other singles, like "I Just Wanna Love U (Give It 2 Me)," kept the album danceable and accessible to his new fans, who just wanted good-time music. The song was produced by the Neptunes and had an infectious Rick James sample in the **hook**. In all there was enough of value that *Dynasty* went double platinum.

## The King of New York

In the years after Notorious B.I.G.'s death, the regional rap feud between coasts had ended. With the passing of Tupac, Death Row had come undone. Dr. Dre had moved on to start Aftermath Records. Snoop Dogg did a brief stint with New Orleans–based No Limit Records. And the CEO of Death Row, Marion "Suge" Knight, had gone to jail. Without Death Row the dominance of West Coast gangsta rap faded, and hip-hop listeners everywhere looked to New York for direction.

As New York became more prominent, a new battle had begun, to decide who would become the most important New York rapper. The unofficial contest began to create hostilities between many New York labels and personalities. Jadakiss from the L.O.X., Queens-based Mobb Deep, Nas, Jay-Z, and DMX all crossed paths in their attempts to become the unchallenged "King of New York." The most notable and most publicized rivalry was between Jay-Z and Nas.

For years the two had coexisted peacefully enough, both mourning the loss of life during the East Coast–West Coast feud and even complimenting each other when the occasion arose. But soon after *The Dynasty* was released, Jay and Nas were trading short jabs on

HIP-HOP ON A HIGHER LEVEL

**XXL**

**JAY-Z**
LEADER OF THE RAP WORLD
★ *President Carter's Cabinet* ★
KANYE WEST
LEBRON JAMES
FOXY BROWN
MEMPHIS BLEEK // YOUNG GUNZ // FREEWAY // PEEDI PEED // DJ CLUE // TEAIRRA MARI

+
PAUL WALL
BUCKSHOT
CLIPSE
*XXL'S 2005*
WHIP PREVIEW

The August 2005 issue of *XXL* magazine pictures Jay-Z with members of Roc La Familia, the rapper's associates on the Roc-A-Fella Records label. Jay-Z's 2000 album *The Dynasty: Roc La Familia* was a collaboration that featured many of these up-and-coming performers.

radio appearances and **mixtapes**. And when Jay went to record his next album, he was ready to take a shot at just about every rapper in New York in order to solidify his position in the industry.

## The Battle for the Crown

*The Blueprint* was released nationwide on Tuesday, September 11, 2001. It was the same morning as the terrorist attacks on the Pentagon and the World Trade Center towers. Despite the mania that gripped the nation after the horrific attacks, *The Blueprint* sold over 450,000 copies by the end of the week, according to SoundScan, a company that monitors music sales.

By 2000, Jay-Z was competing with several rappers for the unofficial title "King of New York." Among his major rivals were Jadakiss, Mobb Deep, Nas, and DMX. The competition launched several feuds, most notably a beef between Nas and Jay-Z.

The album was a critical and commercial success. Jay was praised, with some critics saying that *The Blueprint* was better than *Reasonable Doubt.* Every song except one features Jay-Z alone, silencing the often-voiced complaint that his music relied too heavily on guest artists. He had toned down the sexist lyrics and increased the complexity of his rhyme scheme and subject matter. Jay-Z had created another hip-hop classic.

The album spawned six top singles, none of which could fairly be called fluff: there was one about his mother, one about his legal troubles, another about his regrets concerning relationships with women, and one particularly pointed jab at the hottest rappers in New York at the time. The track "Takeover" used a sample from the classic rock group The Doors and a simple military cadence and bass-line. In the song Jay-Z smears rivals Nas and Prodigy of Mobb Deep, saying that Prodigy had once studied ballet and that Nas had lied about his life before rap. Calling their street credibility into question, Jay asserted himself as the only remaining contender for the "King of New York."

## Jay-Z versus Nas

Few people paid attention when Prodigy answered the barb. He had never been considered a real contender for the crown. Nas, however, had long been considered an artist equal in stature to Jay-Z and Notorious B.I.G. Hip-hop fans were anxious to see how he would respond to Jay-Z's insulting line, "Had a spark when you started, but now you're just garbage."

When Nas answered with his own track, "Ether," it became clear that Jay's insults had riled him. He claimed that Jay was indelicate with B.I.G.'s legacy, rapping: "First, Biggie's your man, then you got the nerve to say that you better than Big . . . " He also suggested that Jay's sexist lyrics were really tied to childhood trauma, and speculated that he might be homosexual. "You seem to be only concerned with dissin' women," Nas teased. "Were you abused as a child, scared to smile, they called you ugly?" It was clearly going to be a fight.

For the next two years, the rappers traded insults on radio stations, concert stages, and through their songs. The beef was watched warily by hip-hop enthusiasts, who did not want to see another conflict with life-and-death consequences. As a response to "Ether," Jay released "Super Ugly," a **freestyle** first aired on the New York radio station Hot

YEAR-END SPECIAL // WINNERS & LOSERS

# Vibe

## NAS & JAY-Z
## THE SHOCKING UNION

PLUS: THE OTHER 42 UNFORGETTABLE
## MOMENTS OF 2005

Nas and Jay-Z are featured on the cover of the January 2006 issue of *Vibe* magazine. The two rappers ended their feud peacefully in 2005, performing songs together at the "I Declare War" concert sponsored by New York radio station Power 105.1.

97 FM, in which he claimed to have had an affair with the mother of Nas's daughter. Many fans found this distasteful. But Jay countered that it was Nas who had crossed the line first.

"Super Ugly" was included on the CD for *Jay-Z Unplugged*, a 2001 MTV production, although the song was not performed during the concert. Backed by The Roots, Jay-Z played the live show in an intimate setting of about 250 people. He did songs from all of his albums and capped the performance with "Takeover."

The beef with Nas died down over the years, although many people still argue who won. Nas never answered "Super Ugly" on record, though he went on radio interviews to condemn Jay-Z's no-holds-barred approach. Jay took another shot at him on his album *The Blueprint 2*, but he left Nas's family out of it, and the beef simply petered out.

Jay-Z poses with a young fan during a ceremony to mark the launch of his signature footwear line, the S. Carter Collection, at a Reebok store in Philadelphia in 2003. Jay-Z has been able to parlay his musical talent into lucrative endorsement deals for many products.

# 6

# Retiring from Rap

Jay-Z's album *The Blueprint 2: The Gift and the Curse* was released in late 2002 to much fanfare. The album was heavily promoted, and sold more than 4 million copies, thanks to singles like "03 Bonnie & Clyde," a duet with his girlfriend Beyoncé Knowles, and "Guns and Roses," which featured Lenny Kravitz.

By now, Jay-Z was so popular that he was offered endorsement deals from several large corporations. One of them, Reebok, would soon present the S. Carter shoe collection, making Jay-Z the first non-athlete to have an athletic shoe named for him. In the first week the shoe was available, the company sold out of its stock. Online bidding wars on sites like eBay quickly set the going rate for a pair at twice their suggested retail price.

Rocawear was also doing quite well, and in 2003 it was valued at over $300 million. The line had been expanded to include women's and children's apparel. Jay had also purchased the U.S. **distribution** rights to a high-end vodka, Armandale, which he and his partners cross-promoted with the music and fashion arms of the Roc-A-Fella empire. Another enterprise was Roc-A-Fella Films, which had produced several successful independent movies, including *Backstage*, *Streets is Watching*, and 2002's *Paid in Full*.

Jay further diversified his business holdings when he opened a trendy sports bar in New York called 40/40 Club in 2003. Two years later, a second 40/40 Club opened in Atlantic City, and Jay was making plans to expand the chain to Los Angeles, Las Vegas, and Singapore.

Things were going well in his personal life also. Though he went out of his way to keep things quiet, he had a new girlfriend, R&B diva Beyoncé Knowles, a wildly successful, multi-platinum recording artist. Some speculate that they had started dating as early as 1999, but neither of them would speak publicly about these rumors.

## Helping Others

Over the years Jay had undertaken a number of philanthropic efforts, such as supporting the New York Mission Society and organizing and funding his annual Jay-Z Santa Claus Toy Drive, in which he takes toys to underprivileged youth at Marcy Houses for the holidays. He also donated to charities related to the September 11 attacks, and performed at the historic Concert For New York. Jay-Z was the only hip-hop artist in the concert. He also donated the proceeds of his November 2003 "retirement" concert to charity.

Although he is satisfied with his meaningful charity work, Jay's proudest moment came when he bought a minority stake in the NBA's New Jersey Nets. He was part of the negotiations to move the team to his hometown of Brooklyn, which will bring jobs, money, and prestige to the embattled borough. "I was happy to cut that check!" he told *Rolling Stone* in 2006.

## Troubling Times

Though Jay was doing well, in the past few years he has also dealt with painful family issues. His mother had insisted on reuniting him with his estranged father, who was dying. Although the relationship between Jay and his father was strained and unpleasant, the two men finally did get some closure. Jay later said, "it was tough. I didn't let him off the hook." Having made peace, Jay was willing to help his

Beyoncé Knowles and Jay-Z attend a fashion show in New York during 2003. Although the two music stars rarely share details of their relationship with the public, it is believed that they began dating in 1999.

In 2003, Jay-Z announced that proceeds from his 2003 Fade to Black concert would be donated to the Hip-Hop Summit Action Network (HSAN). Pictured here are (left to right) HSAN chairman Russell Simmons and president Dr. Ben Chavis, Jay-Z, rapper Reverend Run, and Memphis Bleek.

father. He rented an apartment for him and took care of him financially during the last few months of his life. In 2004, not long after their reunion, his father died.

The following year, Jay was hit with another personal crisis. On June 28, 2005, Jay's youngest nephew was killed in a car accident. Jay had treated the boy like his own son, and his death left Jay an emotional wreck.

Around the same time, tensions were rising between Jay and his Roc-A-Fella co-owners Dash and Burke. They disagreed over the directions the various companies under the Roc-A-Fella umbrella should take. Their management styles and business tactics often differed. Dash, for instance, is known to be hotheaded; he will make quite a fuss when he doesn't get his way. Eventually, the three Roc-A-Fella founders agreed to sell the label to Def Jam.

## Not the Best of Both Worlds

At the same time, Jay-Z was also dealing with problems related to a 2002 album on which he had collaborated with R&B superstar R. Kelly. The two stars had been planning a concert series to promote their album *The Best of Both Worlds*. However, Jay backed out of the shows after R. Kelly was accused of statutory rape and assault.

In 2004, the performers released a second album of material together, *Unfinished Business*. It debuted in the top spot on *Billboard*'s album chart, and a new tour was organized. The tour was billed for 40 cities and was expected to be a huge success, but it eventually fell apart again.

There are varying explanations for why the tour derailed. Some people close to the tour say that Jay was jealous of the greater audience draw that R. Kelly received. Others contend that it was Kelly who was jealous. And still more say there were disagreements about money that were not sorted out before the tour started and later became too deep to manage. Jay maintains that Kelly acted in a consistently unprofessional manner, arriving late and being disrespectful to everyone on staff.

The tour sank on October 29, 2004, at Madison Square Garden when Kelly ran offstage, stopping the show. He claimed that some concertgoers had flashed guns at him. The crowd was searched, and no weapons were recovered. Meanwhile, Kelly claimed, while backstage he and some of his staff were sprayed with pepper spray by a member of Jay's entourage. The entertainers refused to work together after that and went their separate ways. Jay finished the tour with help from guests like Usher and Mary J. Blige.

By early 2005 Jay was ensnared in yet another expensive legal battle, though at least this time he did not face jail. R. Kelly sued him for close to $75 million for lost revenue and damages associated with the ill-fated tour. The case has yet to be settled.

**R&B superstar R. Kelly (left) and Jay-Z speak to the media during a January 2002 press conference for their Best of Both Worlds Tour. Jay-Z eventually fired R. Kelly from the tour, and the R&B star in turn sued the rapper.**

## Onward

In late 2004 Jay started moving on from rap. After Def Jam purchased Roc-A-Fella, he was offered the position of president and chief executive officer (CEO) of the label. As part of his deal with Def Jam, he negotiated for full ownership of his record masters after 10 years. Def Jam still owned them as a result of their initial deal with Roc-A-Fella more than a decade before.

**Jay-Z shows off the four awards he received at the 2004 MTV Video Music Awards ceremony in Miami. He won awards for Best Rap Video, Best Direction in a Video, Best Editing, and Best Cinematography.**

Jay began his new career on New Year's Day 2005 and, despite some disappointments, had a strong first year. He found and developed new performers like Young Jeezy, Rihanna, and Lady Sovereign for Def Jam, while continuing to contribute to the success of veteran Roc-A-Fella acts like Kanye West, currently the biggest star on the label.

Today Jay-Z concentrates his energy on his job at Def Jam and his various other charity and business endeavors. He bought former partner Damon Dash's share in the Rocawear clothing line in 2005 for

**In 2005, Jay-Z took over as president and CEO of Def Jam Recordings. In his new job, he oversees the development of talented new stars for the label. Although he is officially retired from performing, rumors persist that he may one day release another album.**

$30 million, and is currently developing an upscale urban clothing line for the company, the S. Carter Collection. In the spring of 2006, he also lent his name to a watch produced by the Swiss company Audemars Piguet.

Jay-Z is still considered one of the best rappers ever. In fact, a 2006 MTV article named him the "greatest MC of all time." Because of that, many people believe Jay-Z will someday record another hip-hop album. When asked in 2006 whether or not he would record again, Jay told *Rolling Stone*: "I got six or seven good [songs] and a bunch of silly ideas." He admits that he still enjoys and practices rapping, but says it's mainly to entertain himself. "I rhyme more in the shower," he admits. "Every day, every shower."

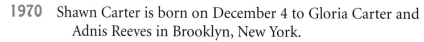

1970   Shawn Carter is born on December 4 to Gloria Carter and Adnis Reeves in Brooklyn, New York.

1982   Adnis Reeves leaves the family home, an event Shawn would later cite as part of the reason he turned to the streets.

1988   Shawn, a neighborhood drug dealer, distinguishes himself as a talented rapper. He records "Hawaiian Sophie" and a video for "The Originators" with Jaz-O, a more established rapper who helps show him the business.

1994   Jay steps into the limelight with superstar rapper Big Daddy Kane, recording a video for "Show and Prove." He continues to hustle drugs.

1995   Jay meets Damon Dash, who signs him to a management deal. They begin to look for a record deal for Jay together.

1996   Jay, Dash, and another associate, Kareem Burke, contribute funds to form Roc-A-Fella Records. Jay's funds come from close to six years of drug sales. *Reasonable Doubt* is released. The album goes gold and will ultimately be hailed as a hip-hop classic. Roc-A-Fella begins negotiations with Def Jam.

1997   Jay's friend Notorious B.I.G. is murdered in Los Angeles. Def Jam and Roc-A-Fella agree to a joint venture, and *In My Lifetime, Vol. 1* is released. The album does well commercially and signifies a move toward a pop audience. Jay retires from the drug business.

1998   Jay releases his biggest hit to date, *Vol. 2: Hard Knock Life.* It will eventually sell more than 5 million copies. He also embarks on a 52-city tour of the same name. Roc-A-Fella Records branches into fashion with the launch of the urban fashion house Rocawear.

1999   Jay releases *Vol. 3: Life and Times of S. Carter,* which garners more critical acclaim than *Vol. 2.* In December Jay is on hand at a New York nightclub when Lance "Un" Rivera is stabbed. He is charged with the stabbing but denies involvement.

2000   *The Dynasty: Roc La Familia,* a compilation album featuring many Roc-A-Fella artists, is released. It sells well but is a critical failure. Jay accepts a plea agreement to avoid jail for his role in Un's stabbing.

**2001** Jay releases *The Blueprint* on September 11, the same morning that terrorist attacks level the World Trade Center and damage the Pentagon. He performs "Izzo (H.O.V.A.)," a single from the album, at the charity event, The Concert for New York. He also impresses listeners with an MTV *Unplugged* performance, backed by players from hip-hop group The Roots.

**2002** Jay releases his first double disc, *The Blueprint 2.* It goes quadruple platinum.

**2003** *The Black Album* is released with much fanfare, as it is Jay-Z's final album. The concert he plans as a good-bye sells out Madison Square Garden in less than five minutes. "99 Problems," a single from the album, wins a Grammy. It sells well and is generally well accepted in both hip-hop and pop circles. Jay-Z retires from his career as an artist officially, though he continues to do shows for the next two years.

**2004** Adnis Reeves dies, having reconciled with Jay. Jay begins negotiations with Warner Music Group and Def Jam Recordings, both of which are offering him an executive post. Jay embarks on tour with R. Kelly, only to have the tour fall apart. Kelly eventually sues him for $75 million. The suit has not been resolved.

**2005** On New Years Day, Jay starts in his new position of president and CEO of Def Jam Recordings. One of Jay's nephews is killed in a car accident in Pennsylvania.

**2006** Jay-Z returns to recording music with his comeback album *Kingdom Come.*

Barbara Walters names Jay-Z as one of the 10 Most Fascinating People of 2006 for his Water For Life project (a collaboration between the United Nations Organisation, MTV, and Def Jam).

# Discography

## Albums

1996  *Reasonable Doubt*

1997  *In My Lifetime, Vol. 1*

1998  *Vol. 2: Hard Knock Life*

1999  *Vol. 3: Life and Times of S. Carter*

2000  *The Dynasty: Roc La Familia*

2001  *The Blueprint*
      *Jay-Z: Unplugged*

2002  *The Best of Both Worlds* (with R. Kelly)
      *The Blueprint 2: The Gift & the Curse*

2003  *The Blueprint 2.1*
      *The Black Album*

2004  *Unfinished Business* (with R. Kelly)
      *Collision Course* (with Linkin Park)

## Top Ten Singles

1998  "Hard Knock Life (Ghetto Anthem)"

1999  "Big Pimpin'"(featuring UGK)

2000  "I Just Wanna Luv U (Give It 2 Me)" (featuring Pharrell Williams)

2001  "Izzo (H.O.V.A.)"

2002  "03 Bonnie & Clyde" (featuring Beyoncé Knowles)

2003  "Excuse Me Miss" (featuring Pharrell Williams)
      "Change Clothes" (featuring Pharrell Williams)

2004  "Dirt Off Your Shoulder"

# Films

1998  *Streets Is Watching*

2000  *Hard Knock Life*

2002  *State Property*
      *Paper Soldiers*

2004  *Fade to Black*

2006  *Diary of Jay-Z: Water for Life*

## Awards Won

1999   *Billboard* Award for Rap Artist of the Year

MTV Video Music Award for Best Rap Video for "Can I Get A . . . "

MTV Video Music Award for Best Video From A Film for "Can I Get A . . . "

2001   Grammy for Best Rap Album for *Vol. 3: Life and Times of S. Carter*

Grammy for Best Rap Performance by Duo or Group for "Big Pimpin'"

Soul Train Award for Sammy Davis Jr. Entertainer of the Year

2002   Grammy for Best Rap Solo Performance for "Izzo (H.O.V.A.)"

Soul Train Award for Album of the Year for *The Blueprint*

2004   American Society of Composers, Authors, and Publishers Award for Golden Note Award

BET Awards for Best Male Hip-Hop Artist

Four MTV Video Music Award for Best Rap Video, Best Direction in a Video, Best Editing, and Best Cinematography.

2005   Grammy for Rap Solo Performance for "99 Problems"

2006   Grammy Award for Best Rap/Sung Collaboration for "Numb/Encore" (with Linkin Park)

Barboza, Craigh. "Friend or Foe?" *USA Weekend* (Jan. 28, 2001).

Boorstin, Julia. "What Makes Damon Dash?" *FSB: Fortune Small Business* 14, no. 7 (September 2004).

Brown, Jake. *Jay-Z and the Roc-a-Fella Records Dynasty*. Phoenix, Ariz.: Amber Books, 2005.

Hira, Nadira A. "America's Hippest CEO." *Fortune* 152, no. 8 (October 2005).

Mayfield, Geoff. "Busy as a Jay-Z." *Billboard* 116, no. 51 (December 18, 2004): p. 49.

Muhammad, Tariq K. "Hip-Hop Moguls: Beyond the Hype." *Black Enterprise* 30, no. 5 (December 1999): p. 78.

Robinson, Lisa. "Beyoncé." *Vanity Fair* 543 (November 2005): p. 337.

Tauber, Michelle, and Lauren Comander. "The Good Life." *People* 62, no. 17 (October 25, 2004).

Toure. "The Book of Jay." *Rolling Stone* 989 (January 2006).

Waddell, Ray. "Worlds Apart." *Billboard* 116, no. 46 (November 13, 2004): p. 1.

## Web Sites

### www.allhiphop.com
This Web site focuses on daily news in the hip-hop world.

### www.jayzfan.info
A fan-operated site dedicated to Jay-Z, with pictures, media, and news updates.

### www.defjam.com
The Web site for Def Jam Recordings contains information and links to Web pages for Jay-Z, as well as other Def Jam and Roc-A-Fella recording artists.

### www.ohhla.com/YFA_jayz.html
A complete collection of Jay-Z's song lyrics, organized by album.

### www.rocafella.com
The Roc-A-Fella Records site features news and history, but also includes transcripts of online chats Jay-Z has hosted since his retirement and other special features.

**boutique**—a small specialty business.

**cross-marketing**—a business practice that involves using one event or product to promote or advertise another. In the case of Roc-A-Fella, for instance, Jay-Z's music helped promote such products as Armandale Vodka and Rocawear apparel.

**dexterity**—skillful and graceful performance or the ability to adjust to changing circumstances without difficulty.

**distribution**—the sale and shipment of records to retail stores.

**freestyle**—once a term used exclusively to describe the act of improvising raps or delivering them off the top of one's head, without writing or even conceptualizing them beforehand. Now, it often refers to a song on a mixtape (as opposed to an album).

**gold**—a record industry designation that an album has sold 500,000 copies.

**hook**—a device in music intended to grab the attention of listeners.

**joint venture**—a partnership between two or more parties that is usually limited to a single enterprise. It involves sharing resources, control, profits, and losses.

**marquee**—having exceptional skill and popularity.

**master**—an original audio recording. Also, a finished recording of the song from which records are pressed and distributed to radio stations and record stores.

**materialistic**—being chiefly concerned with money and that which money can buy.

**misogynistic**—characterized by a hatred of women, often displayed through insults, sexual exploitation, and threats of violence.

**mixtape**—a CD or tape containing authorized or unauthorized tracks from various artists.

**plea agreement**—an deal in which a defendant pleads guilty to a lesser charge and in return the prosecutor drops more serious charges. The prosecutor is assured a conviction, while the defendant is assured a lesser sentence.

**pyrotechnics**—a fireworks display.

**sample**—a portion of previously recorded audio used in a new music piece, which may or may not be from previously released media. Many hip-hop artists use samples heavily.

**subpoena**—a summons that requires a person to appear in court to give testimony. Failure to appear can result in fines or imprisonment.

"03 Bonnie & Clyde" (Jay-Z), 47

"Ain't No Nigga" (Jay-Z), 24
Amil, 40

Bad Boy Entertainment, 26–27
*The Best of Both Worlds* (Jay-Z and R. Kelly), 51
Big Daddy Kane, 18
"Big Pimpin'" (Jay-Z), 36–37
*Black Album* (Jay-Z), 8–9, 13
Blige, Mary J., 10, 51
*The Blueprint 2: The Gift and the Curse* (Jay-Z), 45, 47
*The Blueprint* (Jay-Z), 41, 43
Brown, Foxy, 10, 24, 33
Burke, Kareem ("Biggs"), 13, 23–25, 35, 50, 51
business enterprises, 18, 20–21, 25, 35, 37, 46–48, 51, 54–55

Carter, Gloria (mother), 16
Carter, Shawn. *See* Jay-Z
charity work, 34–35, 48, 50
childhood, 14–17
"The City is Mine" (Jay-Z), 29
Combs, Sean ("Puffy"), 26

Dash, Damon ("Dame"), 10, 13, 18, 20–21, 23–25, 35, 51, 54
Death Row Records, 25–26, 40
Def Jam Recordings, 24, 29–30, 51, 52, 54
DJ Clark Kent, 10, 18, 23
DMX, 33, 34, 40, 42
Dr. Dre, 25, 40
drugs, 16–17, 21
Dupri, Jermaine, 33
*The Dynasty: Roc La Familia* (Jay-Z), 40–41

East Coast–West Coast rap feud, 24–27, 32, 40
Elliott, Missy, 10
"Encore" (Jay-Z), 13
"Ether" (Nas), 43
Evans, Faith, 27

*Fade to Black* (film), 8, 10
Focus on the Family, 33
Freeway, 35
Frey, Glenn, 29

Grammy Awards, 35
"Guns and Roses" (Jay-Z), 47

*Hard Knock Life. See Vol. 2: Hard Knock Life* (Jay-Z)
"Hard-Knock Life (Ghetto Anthem)" (Jay-Z), 32–33
Hip-Hop Summit Action Network (HSAN), 50

*In My Lifetime Vol. 1* (Jay-Z), 28–32

Ja Rule, 33, 34
Jay-Z
    albums, 11, 22–23, 28–35, 36–38, 40–41, 43, 47
    assault arrest, 38–39
    awards won by, 35, 53
    business enterprises, 18, 20–21, 25, 35, 37, 46–48, 51, 54–55
    charity work, 34–35, 48, 50
    childhood, 14–17
    collaborations of, with other artists, 32–34, 40–41, 47
    with Def Jam Recordings, 24, 29–30, 51, 52, 54
    and drugs, 16–17, 21
    early music, 17–19
    and the East Coast–West Coast rap feud, 24–27, 32, 40

family, 48, 50–51
farewell concert, 9–11
as "King of New York," 40–45
and Beyoncé Knowles, 10–11, 13, 47, 48, 49
nickname "Jazzy," 15
and Roc-A-Fella Records, 23–25, 35, 37, 40–41, 51
Jaz-O, 18, 33
"Jazzy." *See* Jay-Z

Kelly, R., 51–52
"King of New York," 40–45
    *See also* Jay-Z
Knight, Marion ("Suge"), 40
Knowles, Beyoncé, 10–11, 13, 17, 47, 48, 49
Kravitz, Lenny, 47

*Life and Times. See Vol. 3: Life and Times of S. Carter* (Jay-Z)
"Lucky Me" (Jay-Z), 30–31
Lyles, Kevin, 10

Marcy Projects, 13, 14–15, 16–17, 34, 48
Memphis Bleek, 13, 33, 34, 40
Method Man, 34
Mobb Deep, 27, 40, 42, 43
MTV Video Music Awards, 53

Nas, 40–45
New Jersey Nets, 48
Notorious B.I.G., 12, 23, 25–27, 29, 43

Original Flavor, 18, 33

?uestlove, 10, 45
Q-Tip, 10, 38

R. Kelly, 51–52
"Rap Game/Crack Game" (Jay-Z), 32
"Real Niggaz" (Jay-Z), 32
*Reasonable Doubt* (Jay-Z), 22–23, 24
Redman, 34
Reeves, Adnis (father), 16, 48, 50
Rivera, Lance ("Un"), 38–39
Roc-A-Fella Films, 48
    *See also* business enterprises
Roc-A-Fella Records, 23–25, 35, 37, 40–41, 51, 54
Rocawear (clothing line), 18, 25, 35, 37, 47–48, 54–55
    *See also* business enterprises
The Roots, 10, 45

S. Carter Collection (footwear), 46, 47, 55
    *See also* business enterprises
Shakur, Tupac, 12, 25–27
Sigel, Beanie, 35, 40
Simmons, Russell, 50
Snoop Dogg, 25, 40
"Super Ugly" (Jay-Z), 43, 45

"Takeover" (Jay-Z), 43
Too $hort, 32

*Unfinished Business* (Jay-Z and R. Kelly), 51

*Vol. 2: Hard Knock Life* (Jay-Z), 32–36
*Vol. 3: Life and Times of S. Carter* (Jay-Z), 36–37

West, Kanye, 54
"Where Have You Been?" (Jay-Z and Beanie Sigel), 40

**Geoffrey Barnes** graduated from Gettysburg College with a degree in philosophy. He currently lives in Portland, Oregon, where he emcees in the band Copacrescent and writes screenplays. This is his first book.

## Picture Credits